Dear Parents:

Congratulations! Your child is taking the first steps on an exciting journey. The destination? Independent reading!

STEP INTO READING® will help your child get there. The program offers five steps to reading success. Each step includes fun stories and colorful art or photographs. In addition to original fiction and books with favorite characters, there are Step into Reading Non-Fiction Readers, Phonics Readers and Boxed Sets, Sticker Readers, and Comic Readers—a complete literacy program with something to interest every child.

Learning to Read, Step by Step!

Ready to Read   Preschool–Kindergarten
• big type and easy words • rhyme and rhythm • picture clues
For children who know the alphabet and are eager to begin reading.

Reading with Help   Preschool–Grade 1
• basic vocabulary • short sentences • simple stories
For children who recognize familiar words and sound out new words with help.

Reading on Your Own   Grades 1–3
• engaging characters • easy-to-follow plots • popular topics
For children who are ready to read on their own.

Reading Paragraphs   Grades 2–3
• challenging vocabulary • short paragraphs • exciting stories
For newly independent readers who read simple sentences with confidence.

Ready for Chapters   Grades 2–4
• chapters • longer paragraphs • full-color art
For children who want to take the plunge into chapter books but still like colorful pictures.

STEP INTO READING® is designed to give every child a successful reading experience. The grade levels are only guides; children will progress through the steps at their own speed, developing confidence in their reading. The F&P Text Level on the back cover serves as another tool to help you choose the right book for your child.

Remember, a lifetime love of reading starts with a single step!

To my grandma, Leona Manning,
and her great-grandchildren
—A.M.

To Julia
—T.B.

Text copyright © 2017 by Anna Membrino
Cover art and interior illustrations copyright © 2017 by Tim Budgen

All rights reserved. Published in the United States by Random House Children's Books, a division of Penguin Random House LLC, New York.

Step into Reading, Random House, and the Random House colophon are registered trademarks of Penguin Random House LLC.

Visit us on the Web!
StepIntoReading.com
randomhousekids.com

Educators and librarians, for a variety of teaching tools, visit us at RHTeachersLibrarians.com

Library of Congress Cataloging-in-Publication Data is available upon request.

ISBN 978-0-399-55728-6 (trade) — ISBN 978-0-399-55729-3 (lib. bdg.) — ISBN 978-0-399-55730-9 (ebook)

Printed in the United States of America
20 19 18
First Edition

This book has been officially leveled by using the F&P Text Level Gradient™ Leveling System.

Big Shark, Little Shark

by Anna Membrino

illustrated by Tim Budgen

Random House 🏠 New York

Big shark.

Little shark.

5

Big Shark has
big teeth.

Little Shark has
little teeth.

Big Shark
swims fast.

Little Shark

swims slow.

Big Shark is hungry.
It is time
for a snack!

10

Big Shark sees
a little fish.

The little fish
swims fast.

Big Shark

swims fast, too.

Big Shark goes CHOMP!

But the little fish
is too fast!

No snack for
Big Shark.

17

Big Shark

swims slow.

Little Shark
swims fast.

Little Shark is hungry.

It is time

for a snack!

Little Shark sees
a BIG fish.

The big fish goes CHOMP!

Swim faster,
Little Shark!

The big fish is gone!

Little Shark
is still hungry.

Little Shark sees
Big Shark.

Big Shark

is still hungry.

Uh-oh.

Wait!

Little Shark has a net.